TOP HA
Stack no. 4
Railway Tu
Only Star
raised whe
Tries to av
dirty work

CW00840052

WARRIOR
Stack no. 5 –
Harbour Tug
Very strong, but
sometimes clumsy.
Will tackle any job.

HERCULES
Stack no. 6 – Ocean-
going Tug
One of the leaders of
the fleet. Very proud
and rather aloof.

SUNSHINE
Stack no. 7 –
Harbour Switcher
Newest member of
the Star Fleet. Works
mainly with Ten
Cents.

TITLES AVAILABLE IN BUZZ BOOKS

First published 1990 by Buzz Books,
an imprint of the Octopus Publishing Group,
Michelin House, 81 Fulham Road, London, SW3 6RB.

LONDON MELBOURNE AUCKLAND

Text © 1990 William Heinemann Ltd

Illustrations © 1990 William Heinemann Ltd
Story by Fiona Hardwick
Illustrations by The County Studio
Based on the television series TUGS produced by TUGS Ltd
for Clearwater Features (1986) Ltd and TVS Television,
© TUGS 1988.
All rights reserved

ISBN 1 85591 013 6

Printed and bound in the UK by BPCC Paulton Books Ltd.

• A TUGS ADVENTURE •

RUN AGROUND

Story by Fiona Hardwick
Illustrations by The County Studio

buzz books

One day, Captain Zero called a meeting of
the Z Stacks.

"Right, you lot," he said. "We're not
doing enough business – so get out there
and find it! I don't care how you do it!"

Zorran scowled angrily.

"It's those rotten Star Tugs that are the problem – bunch of creeps, the lot of 'em," he muttered to himself. Then he had a great idea. An evil grin spread across his face and he looked around for someone to help him.

"Come here, Zug!" he shouted.

"Yes, Zorran what is it? Have you got a job for me?" said Zug, steaming up beside the head of the Z Stacks.

"Aren't we clever this morning?" sneered Zorran. "Listen carefully and do exactly what I tell you . . ."

Later, Zug found Big Mac in the harbour. He was very scared of the big tug, and tried to sound calm as he said:

"Um, hold on Big Mac. Captain Star says you must go to the disused docks and c . . . collect a c . . . coal barge urgently."

8

Big Mac frowned and Zug gulped
nervously. Big Mac wasn't convinced.

"Humph," he said. "I'll telephone the
Captain on my way, to check."

But then he met Hercules, and somehow,
the telephone call was forgotten.

"Oi, Sunshine!" yelled Zorran later.
"Big Mac needs some help at the disused
docks. Can't think why he'd choose you."

"Oh, right. I'd better report back to
Star Pier first, though," said Sunshine.

"Well, if you can't be bothered, I'll send
one of my tugs down there," jeered Zorran.

10

Zorran and Zug sniggered together.

"With Big Mac and Sunshine 'busy' at the disused docks, those Star Tugs can't steal all our work – and we'll make the money instead!" said Zorran.

"Who's next?" asked Zug. "Shall I tell Warrior he's needed at the docks too?"

11

"Warrior? That clumsy oaf?" hissed Zorran. "Oh no — we can leave him to mess things up for the Star Tugs on his own!"

Warrior was the clumsiest tug in the harbour. He tried to help, but when he was around, things had a habit of going wrong!

Much later, Sunshine and Big Mac came into the harbour, looking very angry.

"Sorry, Captain. We were tricked! When I find that Zorran I'll . . . I'll . . ."

"I've told you before, tugs. I'm Captain here, and I give the orders!"

Sunshine hated letting the Captain down.

"Never mind this time, Sunshine," said
Captain Star. "Remember though –
Lillie Lightship needs an urgent oil delivery
first thing tomorrow. She's very low, but
she's got enough for tonight. She'll need it,
with this storm coming up."

But, out in the estuary, Lillie was in big trouble. As the rough sea tossed her from side to side, her last drum of oil fell over and slithered into the sea. The oil left in her light burned away; then there was darkness.

"How terrible!" said Lillie. "What shall I do now?"

The weather got worse. A huge freighter
making its way up the estuary looked for
Lillie's light to guide her past the rocks.

Desperately, Lillie sounded her foghorn in
warning, but the strong winds carried away
the sound.

16

The freighter slid on to the rocks with a horrible crunch, and keeled over to one side, completely stuck.

A little later, Zug saw the red light of distress signals in the sky.

"I'd better go and see what's wrong."

Zug found the stranded freighter and sped back for help.

"Zorran, listen," he spluttered, "there's a freighter in the estuary . . . stuck on rocks . . . and Lillie Lightship's gone out!"

"Oh yes, and I suppose the sea's turned pink!" snarled Zorran. "You can't fool me with that game – I thought of it, you little idiot, remember?"

"No, no it's the truth – really!" pleaded poor Zug.

"Scram! I haven't got time for your stupid jokes!"

Zorran turned and went off in the opposite direction.

Zug didn't know what to do. Then he spotted Warrior. Although he was clumsy, Warrior was also strong and very helpful.

"Warrior . . ." began Zug.

"What is it, Zug?" Even Warrior had heard about Big Mac and Sunshine, so he had no time for Z Stacks.

"Look, you won't believe this . . ."

"Probably not," snapped Warrior.

"Please, Warrior this isn't a trick, honest.
There's a freighter out there trapped on the
rocks. I can't manage it, but I thought we
could bring her in together."

Warrior still looked very suspicious.

"I know we played that stupid trick. It was all Zorran's idea and now *he* won't believe me. Please help rescue the freighter – it'll be your salvage."

"All right Zug, I'll do it – but if this is another trick, you'll be sorry!"

Warrior and Zug set off together to find the freighter.

She wasn't too badly damaged, but spending a night buffeting about on the treacherous rocks would destroy her.

"This is going to be tough," said Warrior.

He revved his engine up to full power and
pushed with all his strength to get the
freighter off the rocks. Zug helped to steady
her as she listed in the water.

"Hold on Zug, while I connect a line,"
gasped Warrior.

Slowly, very slowly, Warrior and Zug
brought the freighter into the harbour,
where she could dock before being taken to
Lucky's Yard in the morning.

The Star Tugs gathered round to
congratulate them.

"Well done, Warrior!"

"You saved the day!"

Everyone was full of praise for Warrior – Captain Star included. Warrior beamed.

"Young Zug here did his bit, too," he said, blushing modestly.

Hearing Zug's name, Zorran pushed in.

"What d'you think you're doing, helping Star Tugs?"

"But Zorran, I tried to tell you about the freighter – oh, oh, look out, Zorran behind you!" squealed Zug.

"I've told you once, no more tricks, you miserable little squirt. When Captain Zero hears . . . AAARGH!!"

27

WARRIOR

Warrior had got too excited, and as he sped round the harbour, an enormous wave splashed over Zorran. His wheelhouse was completely waterlogged.

"Oh, I'm SO sorry," grinned Warrior.

And even Zug couldn't help joining in as they all laughed at Zorran.

THE Z STACKS

ZORRAN
Stack no. 1 –
Harbour Tug
Leader of the Z
Stacks. A mean,
tough character.

ZEBEDEE
Stack no. 2 –
Harbour Tug

ZAK
Stack no. 3 –
Harbour Tug